CREATURES HUNT

OCTOPUS & CRAB

A family game: Two crabs are inside their home. They hear a knock on the door. 'Who's there? ' they ask. 'Crab,' says a voice, so they open the door but to their surprise an octopus comes inside. One crab runs to the left. Another crab runs to the right. Octopus has to pick which direction it should go to eat, and it swiftly catches a treat... but in the end through tears of sadness (or a kiss - because that tends to make everything better) those who perish always come back to life.

My son Lucian and I would play this game all the time and so I dedicate this book to him.

And to my adorable son Niko as I'll never forget your first gut-busting laughter that happened with Lucian lunging a stuffed octopus into your belly over and over.

— Love, Mom

To my son Lucian, who helped expand the limits of my imagination.
To my son Nikolas, who showed me that one can love again.

— Love, Dad

Color by Bruna Franceschini

First edition.

ISBN 978-1-7360448-3-4

Tupelo Books
visit us at www.tupelobooks.com

CREATURES HUNT

OCTOPUS & CRAB

ERINNISSE & PATRYK REBISZ

TUPELO BOOKS

It’s not very deep in the ocean,
where the Octopus sleeps in a cave.

The perfect hideaway;
a dark and calm lair
that the Octopus furnished
from rocks found near the shore.

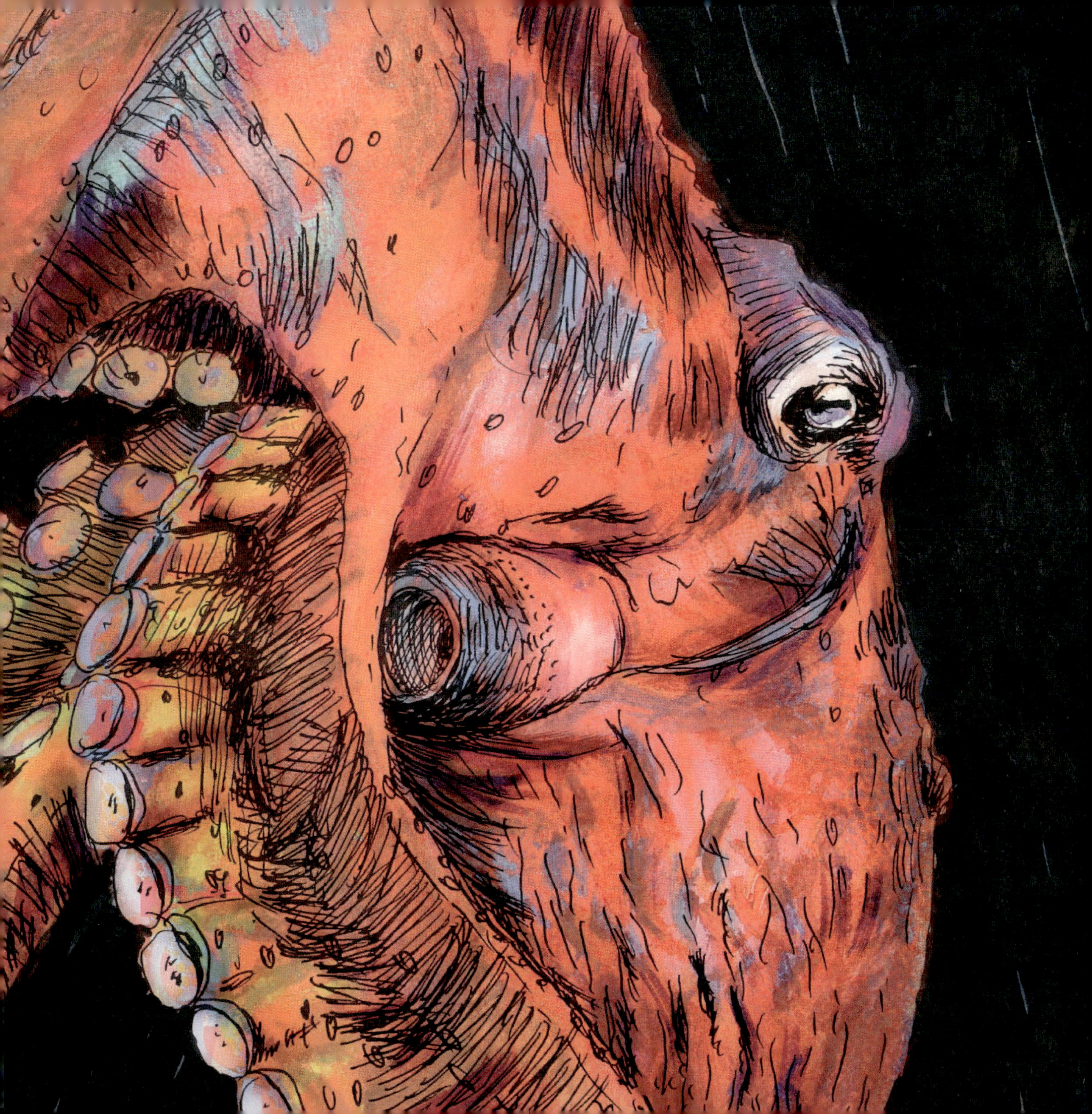

Famished, after a long sleep,
the Octopus needs to eat.

How does the Octopus eat?
It has a beak hidden underneath.
(Really! It looks just like a parrot's.)

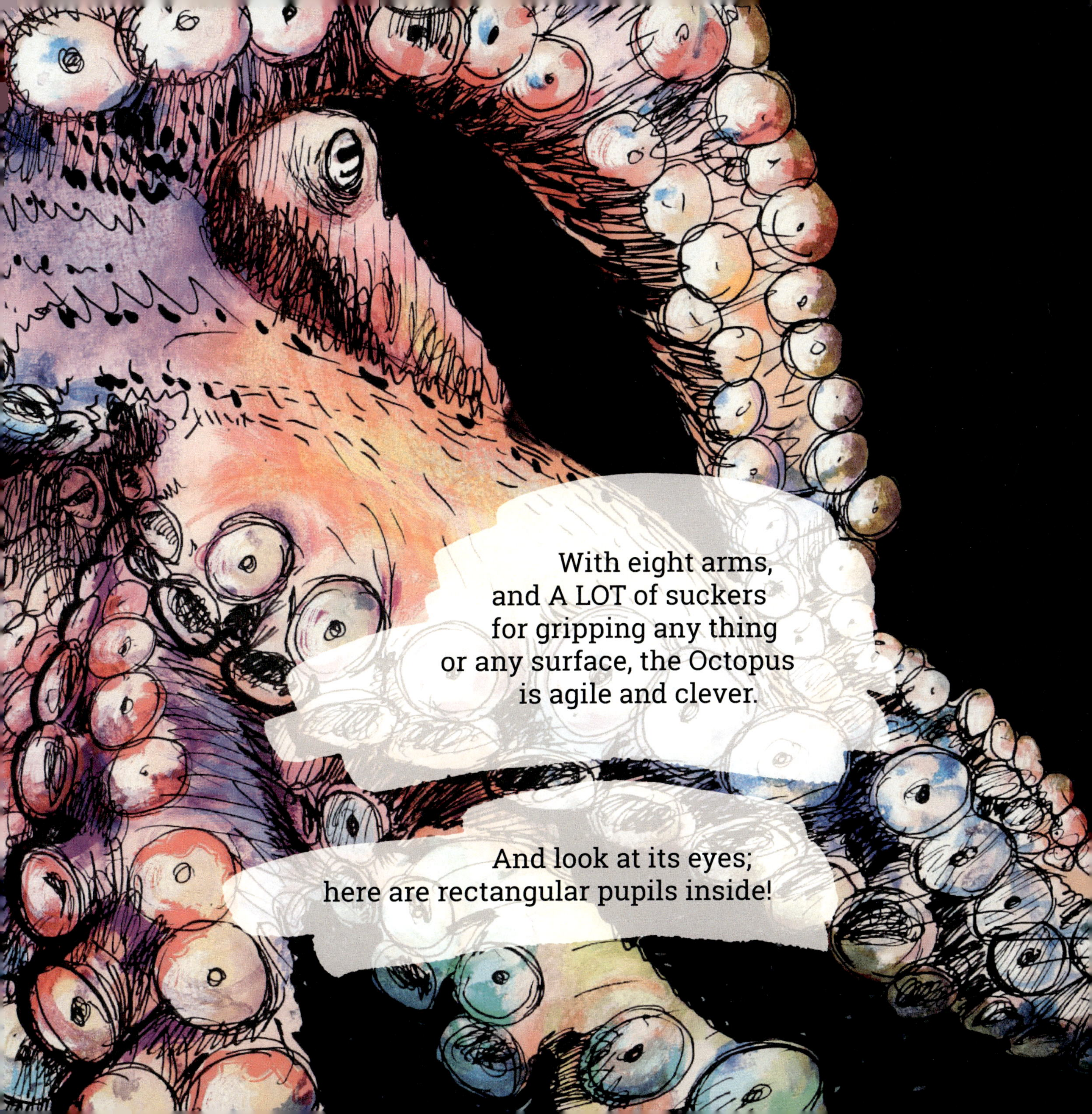

With eight arms,
and A LOT of suckers
for gripping any thing
or any surface, the Octopus
is agile and clever.

And look at its eyes;
here are rectangular pupils inside!

Amazing and true,
the Octopus skin can change color too.
Any color you can see... **Wait!**

Where did it go?

Close to the shore,
where it's not too deep,
the Crab walks sideways
along the ocean floor.

The Crab has many legs, and a very hard shell.
Its two strong pincer claws
easily grab and break
whatever is within reach.

Look over here.
A fish!

But, the fish is too fast and swims away,
so the Crab waddles sideways
and eats some algae instead.

Finding some barnacles stuck to a large rock, the Crab gulps down a loose one...

Then pries off another one, but as it reaches for a third...

In the blink of an eye,
with its tentacles open wide...

CRUNCH!
goes the crab.

A scrumptious snack,
but the Octopus must look for more.

Who eats you?

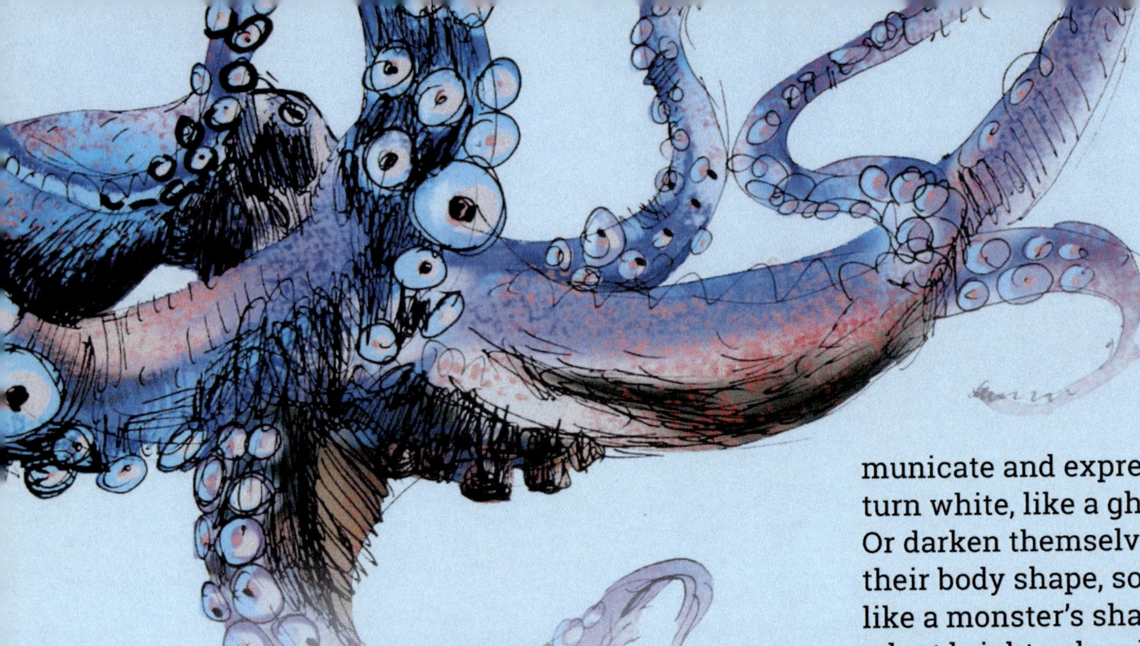

OCTOPUS FACTS:

An octopus is an invertebrate. An invertebrate is a creature without a spine. (Do you know where your spine is?) The fact is, octopuses don't have any bones, which is what allows them to have their amazing abilities to change their body's thickness and shape.

Everyone knows how many tentacles an octopus has... Eight, of course! Two of these are used as legs and the other six are used for arms. Additionally, the octopus's skin changes color. Octopuses can even turn bumpy, smooth, or even spikey. They are well-known masters of camouflage, but there is something else scientists continue to study and decipher: how the octopus uses color to communicate and express emotions. They turn white, like a ghost, when frightened. Or darken themselves while expanding their body shape, so they loom large like a monster's shadow. They also can adopt bright colored spots or rings which triggers other animals to believe they are poisonous to eat. (This is a survival trick that many creatures possess, it's called aposematism.)

Their suckers, not only help them grip and grab, but also are how an octopus tastes and smells!

Octopuses are part of the mollusk family of sea creatures. (Try saying 'mollusk' eight times!) Other examples of mollusks are snails, squids and cuttlefish. Another fun octopus-related word is a cephalopod, which names those creatures that squirt black ink. When an octopus wants to escape danger, or confuse another creature, it will shoot black ink that billows around the threat like a dark cloud. This allows the octopus to launch itself backwards and disappear.

CRAB FACTS:

A crab is a decapod - meaning it has ten legs with one set made of pincers. Generally, the other four pairs are walking legs, but some crabs have swimmerets for the last pair which they use as a shovel and to swim. They easily travel forwards and backwards, but crabs move fastest when they travel sideways.

Crabs are referred to as "spiders of the sea" because of their segmented legs. They are similar to spiders in one other way too - they both have skeletons on the outside of their body. This is called an exoskeleton. For a crab to grow bigger it must molt, which means it will shed its shell, then grow bigger with a new shell. And if a crab were to lose a leg or claw, it will grow back with time.

The largest crab in the world is the Japanese spider crab. It has a leg span of up to 13 feet, which is more than two adults lying feet to feet. Pea crabs are the smallest. (Can you guess how small they are?)

Crab eyes are amazing. They are made of thousands of little lenses and can see 360 degrees around them (which means they can see behind themselves without turning!). Their eyes, on a stem that grows out of their body, are even able to pop-up through the sand. When a crab hides, it will scan its surroundings like a periscope on a submarine.

Crabs work in teams to source food and protect each other. They are omnivores, which means they eat meat and plants. But more so, they are better known for being scavengers. Crabs have teeth, but some don't have teeth in their mouth - they have them in their stomach! As a community, they communicate with each other through drumming sounds and signaling flaps of their pincer claws. You can find a crab living almost anywhere in the ocean, even near deep-sea volcanoes.

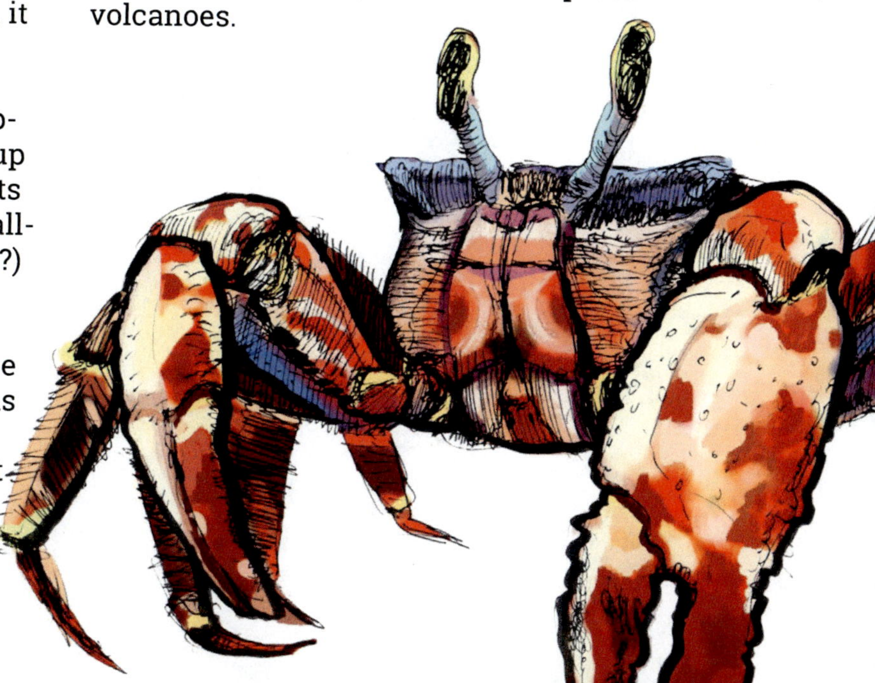

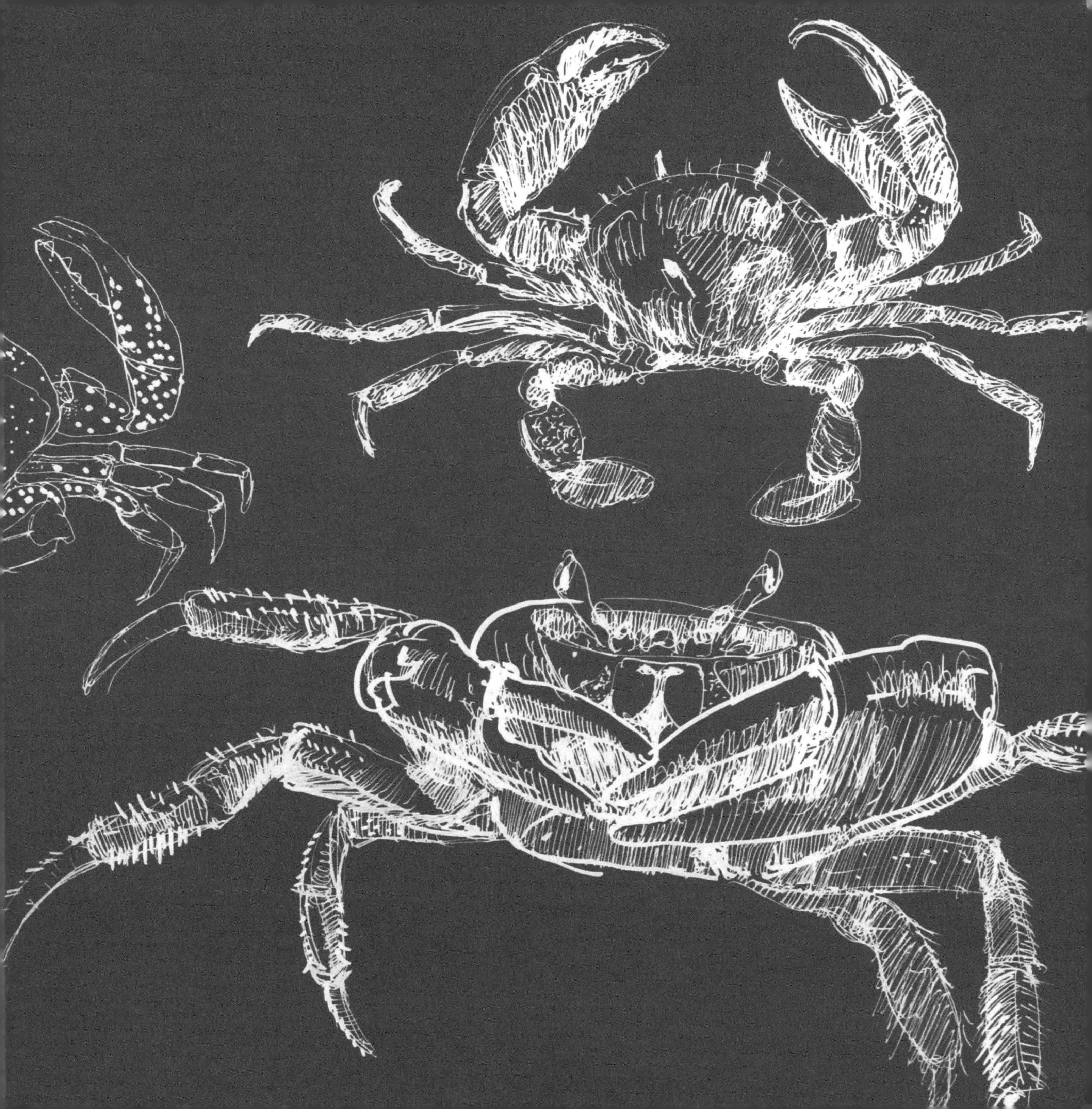

Made in the USA
Middletown, DE
29 November 2021